For Alden and Lennox

RUFUS & BEA

LISA TUCKER CUMMINS and RYAN CUMMINS
Illustrated by HANNAH PASCOE

On the low-hanging branch of an ancient oak,
hovering just above a fragrant patch of wildflowers,
is a nest made of leaves and grass.
In it sits a small songbird in a red trapper hat.

Meet Rufus Nightingale.

Oh, what's this?
It appears our new friend is about to sing!
Let's listen, shall we?

"LA LA LACCKK ACKK!" Rufus coughs.
"LA LA LA *SCREEEECH!*" Rufus squeaks.

Hmm . . . it looks like Rufus hasn't found his song quite yet. Well, that's all right. He's new at this.

With a sigh, Rufus flops down in his nest.

Have you ever wished for a thing to come true,
but making it happen seemed too hard to do?

Then perhaps you'll relate to our young feathered friend,
whose grand songbird dreams have him at his wit's end.

Or so he thinks, with hopes locked in suspension.
And that's when a strange buzz catches his attention.

Rufus leans out of his nest just far enough to spot a happy bunch of bees pollinating the wildflowers below. He listens as the sound of singing drifts his way . . .

I can play kazoo, and you can too.
I can play kazoo, and you can too.
Bzzzzz bzzz b-bzz b-bzzzz b-bzzzz-bzzzz-bzzzzzz!

Enchanted by the music, Rufus leans farther over the edge of his nest.

Suddenly—*snap!*—some twigs break loose!

Rufus flutters his wings and scrambles to keep from falling.

Down below, his red trapper hat and bits of his nest crash to the ground!

The bees stop buzzing and look up. But then they continue with their work.

All but one, that is . . .

An inquisitive little honeybee flies up to the nest, where she finds Rufus.

"Excuse me, but I think this may belong to you," she says.

"Um, yeah, thank you," Rufus says bashfully.

"You're welcome!" she exclaims. "By the way, I'm Beatrix Bedelia Blossom! But you can call me 'Bea.' Coincidentally, I'm also a *bee*. What's your name?"

"I'm Rufus Nightingale. It's nice to meet you, Bea the bee!"

"Pleasure to meet you, Rufus! Also, I do want to note that our hive has gone 365 days without a single accident on the job, so if you could kindly prevent any additional objects from falling from the sky, that would be appreciated."

"Sorry! I got distracted listening to your song," he replies.

"You're a songbird, right?" asks Bea. "Why didn't you join us?"

"Because I don't exactly know how to sing," Rufus admits.

"Well, that's OK," Bea assures him. "Would you like to fly down and we'll teach you?"

"That would be amazing!" he exclaims. "But . . . I don't know how to fly yet, either."

"Wait . . . you're a *songbird* who doesn't know how to *sing* or *fly*?"

Rufus looks down and nods without saying a word.

"HOW EXCITING!"
says Bea.

"I remember when I first learned how to fly . . .
The liftoff! The not-plummeting-helplessly through the air!
And the flying—that's really the best part, the *flying*!" Bea
buzzes enthusiastically.

"I can only imagine!" replies Rufus in wonder.

"Would you like me to teach you to fly too?!" offers Bea.

"Would I ever!" Rufus declares.

"BEEEEEA-U-TIFUL!"

"OK, my soon-to-be-singing-and-flying songbird friend,"
Bea begins. "Tell me, what happens when you try?"

"Well . . ." Rufus takes a deep breath.
"I guess when I think about singing,
I think about how I want it to sound.
And then I think about how it *actually* sounds
and what others will think.
And then I think about how *I'm* thinking about it,
and then . . ."

"I think we've found our problem, songbird. The secret to singing is to *not* think about singing," Bea explains.

Rufus raises his head to look at Bea. "Huh?"

"You don't have to impress. Just express," Bea answers.

She steps on the edge of the nest as though stepping in front of a massive crowd.
"Friends, roses, country hens!
Lend me your ears!"

Bea clears her throat and begins to softly sing:

♪ *You don't have to sing.* ♪
You only have to speak.
And when your words come out,
they sound so pretty.

"I think I can do that," says Rufus.

"Wonderful! Join me," Bea encourages him.

Rufus and Bea begin singing together:

>   *You don't have to sing.*
>   *You only have to speak.*
>   *And when your words come out,*
>   *they sound so pretty.*

"This is fun!" Rufus exclaims.

"You're doing great! Now, just feel it!" says Bea.

The two take turns before singing the last line together.

♫ *You don't have to sing.* ♪
But if you want, please do.
Choose any song you like . . .
And we will sing with you!
♪ ♫

"Did I just sing my first song?" asks Rufus.

Bea can't help but smile. "I think so, songbird. But that's not all. Look!"

"Well, look at that: the nest is gone—the nest is *gone*?" Rufus exclaims.
"Wait, am I flying?!"

"Sure looks like it to me," says Bea.

"Oh my gosh, I'm flying!

I'M FLYING!" Rufus cheers.

"Flying *and* singing," Bea reminds him. "You're a bona fide songbird!"

"I couldn't have done it without your help, Bea," Rufus responds.

"Sure, you could've," replies Bea, "but sometimes things are easier with the help of a friend."

So a friendship was born between the bird and the bee,
a pairing quite likely to give many glee.
Their laughter so joyful. Their stories sublime.
And we'll share some more when we see you next time!

THE END
(For now.)

Music & Lyrics

"YOU DON'T HAVE TO SING"

You don't have to sing.
You only have to speak.
And when your words come out,
they sound so pretty.

You don't have to sing.
You only have to speak.
And when your words come out,
they sound so pretty.

[Kazoo & bird whistle]

You don't have to sing.
But if you want, please do.
Choose any song you like . . .
And we will sing with you!

"I CAN PLAY KAZOO"

I can play kazoo, and you can too!
I can play kazoo, and you can too!
Bzzzzz bzzz b-bzz b-bzzzz b-bzzzz-bzzzz-bzzzzzz!

[Kazoo]

Find the official soundtrack to Rufus & Bea by Tiny Prime anywhere you listen to music.

This is a work of fiction. Names, characters, organizations, places, events, and incidents are either products of the author's imagination or are used fictitiously.

Copyright © 2024 by Ryan and Lisa Cummins
All rights reserved.

No part of this book may be reproduced, or stored in a retrieval system, or transmitted in any form or by any means, electronic, mechanical, photocopying, recording, or otherwise, without express written permission of the publisher.

Tiny
Prime

Created by Tiny Prime
www.TinyPrime.com

Published by Flashpoint Books™, Seattle
www.flashpointbooks.com

Produced by Girl Friday Productions

Design: Paul Barrett
Production editorial: Laura Dailey
Project management: Mari Kesselring

ISBN (hardcover): 978-1-959411-58-1
ISBN (ebook): 978-1-959411-59-8

Library of Congress Control Number: 2023952477

First edition